DILLO

A BABY ARMADILLO'S ADVENTURE ON SANIBEL ISLAND

By Kyle L. Miller

Jungle House
Publications
Sanibel Island, Florida
2005

To Finn and Beckett
Happy Reading?!
Kyle L. Miller
March 23, 2012

Written by Kyle L. Miller
junglehousepublications@yahoo.com

Illustrated by Randon T. Eddy
Randon T. Studios, Sanibel, FL
www.Randontstudio.com

Graphic design and Layout by Franziska Krauss
frenchykdesign@yahoo.com

ISBN-13: 978-0-9769332-0-5
ISBN-10: 0-9769332-0-9
Library of Congress Control Number: 2005904903

Map of Sanibel Island, Florida, courtesy of U. S. Fish & Wildlife Service

Printed in China

Jungle House Publications
736 Cardium St.
Sanibel Island, FL 33957
(239) 472-0599
junglehousepub@yahoo.com
www.junglehousepublications.com

Acknowledgments

I would like to extend special thanks to several individuals whose input and encouragement helped to make this book become a reality. My dear friend, the writer Robert J. Cronin, gave me the inspiration to write a story about island animals. Bev Postmus, a master naturalist and well-respected authority on birds, contributed her expert advice on the accuracy of the environmental and wildlife descriptions in the Bailey Tract Refuge. I want to give special thanks to my friend the writer Dr. Sidney B. Simon, whose invaluable skill with editing helped to animate life into the characters and bring a storytelling flow to Dillo's adventure. A very special thanks goes to my dear friend, Randon T. Eddy, whose encouragement and enthusiasm for this story made the entire process pure joy. Randon's artistic illustrations throughout the book not only make the story come to life visually but make the book a work of art as well. I also want to thank Franziska Krauss, whose exceptional abilities and dedication to her art produced the layout and graphics for this book. It is my great fortune to know and give thanks to professor and author Anne Fadiman for the time she generously spent proofreading this book. No creative project I have attempted would be complete without expressing gratitude to my dear sister, Alice Miller Masci, for her ongoing unconditional love and support.

Roosevelt Channel

Captiva Island

Buck
Key

Runyon Key

Wulfert Keys

Pine Island Sound

Hard Working Bayou

Wulfert Keys
Trail

Shell Mound
Trail

Wildlife Drive

Indigo Trail

Sanibel-Captiva Rd

N
W
E
S

Gulf Of Mexico

Sanibel Island
Florida

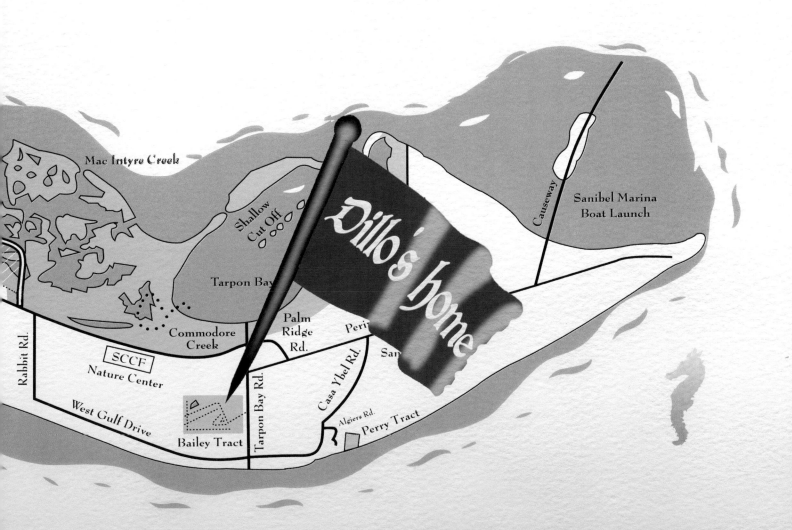

Mac Intyre Creek

Shallow Cut Off

Tarpon Bay

Commodore Creek

SCCF
Nature Center

Rabbit Rd.

West Gulf Drive

Bailey Tract

Tarpon Bay Rd.

Palm Ridge Rd.

Peri

Casa Ybel Rd.

Sar

Algiers Rd.

Perry Tract

Dillo's home

Causeway

Sanibel Marina
Boat Launch

Dedication

This book is dedicated to my four wonderful grandchildren, Cooper, Nikala, Allyson, and Madison, and all of the children in the world who can make a difference for the future protection of wildlife and the preservation of wildlife environment.

With all my love, Grand-Ma K

Contents

J. N. Ding Darling National Wildlife Refuge

Bailey Tract

Bailey Tract is a 100-acre freshwater wildlife preserve located on Sanibel Island, off the southwest coast of Florida. It is included as a part of the 6,300-plus-acre J. N. Ding Darling National Wildlife Refuge. The Tract has walking trails that go around many ponds, through wetlands, and along a river.

There is a wide variety of wildlife that can be found in the Bailey Tract. Bobcats, raccoons, armadillos, opossums, river otters, marsh rabbits, and many species of mice and rats are among the mammals that live in the Tract.

Reptiles include alligators, lizards, skinks, and many species of snakes, turtles, frogs, and toads.

A very large variety of birds and water fowl can also be found in the Bailey Tract. Blue-winged teals, mottled ducks, common moorhens, American coots, black-necked stilts, great and snowy egrets, tricolored herons, white ibis, anhingas, and green and blue herons are most common. Nesting birds include red-shouldered hawks, red-bellied woodpeckers, great crested flycatchers, northern mockingbirds, white-eyed vireos, and red-winged blackbirds. Many warblers, sparrows, blackbirds, catbirds, and cardinals can also be found in the thick brush in the Tract. Osprey nests are found near the Tract, since they often feed on fish in the ponds.

Vegetation in the Bailey Tract consists of spartina grass, cordgrass, saw grass, cattails, and leather ferns in the marsh areas. Common trees include cabbage palms, strangler figs, and buttonwoods. Common brush species are the saltbush and the wax myrtle.

Bailey Tract is where the story of Dillo takes place.

The Bailey Tract

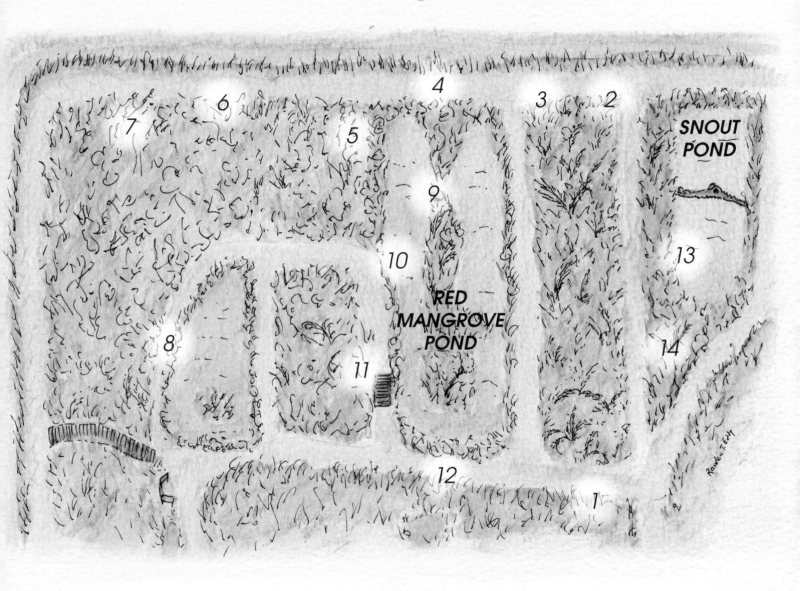

- 1 -
Dillo's Birth

*I*t was a sound of pain, "EEEEEEEEE," that came from a hole in the ground under a lichen-covered log in the Bailey Tract wildlife preserve. The sun was just rising, but Marmma Armadillo didn't care. "EEEEEEEE," she cried again. She was deep down under ground in her nest, giving birth to the last of four identical baby girls. Armadillos always give birth to four identical babies because they all come, amazingly, from one egg split in four. The first three babies were born easily and already pushing into Marmma's tummy for their first meal. This last baby was having a very hard time coming into the world.

"EEEEEEEEE," she cried again, and finally the baby was born into her new home.

After this difficult birth, Marmma was very relieved to see that her fourth baby was born alive. She began to lick and clean all of the babies. She was so happy to be a new mother. She didn't care if they were boys or girls, just as long as they were healthy. As she cleaned the first baby, she said, "You will be called '**Lillo.**'" She named the second baby "**Pillo**" and the third baby "**Jillo.**" After each baby was cleaned, it scrambled to her tummy for more food. She finally got to the last baby and noticed that it seemed to be larger than the other three babies.

"I guess that's why you had trouble squeezing out," she said as she took special care to lick and clean it. Marmma checked carefully for any problems that might have occurred during her birth.

"You will be called '**Dillo,**'" she said as she licked Dillo's little face clean. Then she noticed that something about her was different from the other girls. "Oh, my goodness," Marmma said as she looked at the baby. Dillo was looking up at her mother with a big smile on her face. It seems that the pressure of birth had affected some nerves in her face and she was born with, of all things, a permanent smile. Marmma's reaction was, "Well, don't you look cute."

Dillo just smiled, and smiled some more. Then she tried to squirm in between her sisters to get her first meal. Life in the new world did not start out well for Dillo, because her sisters kept kicking her away from Marmma's tummy so they could have all the milk.

Marmma soon noticed that Dillo was not getting fed and pulled Lillo, Jillo, and Pillo away from her tummy so Dillo could eat. And since they wouldn't let Dillo eat with them, Marmma took special care to make sure Dillo ate first. The sisters did not like that one bit. And they didn't like the fact that Dillo looked so different. She just kept smiling, and they couldn't.

When only one day had passed, the baby armadillos were ready to explore the world outside of their sandy burrow under the cabbage palm tree log. Marmma walked cautiously out of the nest with her babies close beside her. She looked and sniffed all around to see if it was safe for the babies to be out of the burrow. The four babies all sniffed the air around them to take in the new odors of their surroundings. Then Marmma began her first lesson on where the girls could find the best food.

"There are many things we can find to eat out here in the Bailey Tract. There are spiders and grasshoppers above the ground, and ants, beetles, and yummy worms under the ground. One day I will take you to the water for snails and frogs. But for now, you must stay close to me and we will go exploring. Don't go too far from me," Marmma warned. "There are many dangers in the marshland that you don't know about yet."

Marmma's lessons for her young armadillos continued for several weeks. Then one day Marmma said, "OK, girls, you are now ready to venture out on your own. Just make sure you know where I am all the time."

Happily, Lillo, Jillo, and Pillo set out to explore without Marmma. Dillo did not want to go with her sisters since they were not nice to her, but she didn't want to look like a "Marmma's girl" either. So she followed at a safe distance behind her sisters. The sisters walked past a large gray mound of sand. Dillo knew they didn't see it and exclaimed with excitement, "Look, a nest of ants!" She thought that sharing the sweet ants would make her sisters like her.

"Oh, boy," shouted Lillo as she turned to look at the ant hill.

"Let's go!" said Pillo.

"Yummy!" said Jillo, running to the ant nest with her sisters.

And with that, Lillo, Jillo, and Pillo scurried over to where Dillo had found the treasure of ants. They rudely pushed her out of the way and began scratching the ground to eat the ants that were angrily emerging out of their nest.

"Girls!" scolded Marmma from a short distance away. "Let Dillo eat, too! After all, she found those ants for you."

"Never mind," said Dillo, lowering her smiling face. She was angry and disappointed at the same time, and she really didn't feel like smiling, but the smile wouldn't go away. "I will find some more ants," she said to Marmma.

Marmma knew, in spite of her smile, that Dillo was upset. She felt sorry for her sad, smiling baby and said, "Come with me, Dillo, I'll help you find some scrumptious worms."

Dillo really wanted to find her own worms, but didn't want to offend her mother, so she followed Marmma beneath a salt bush to rummage through the dead leaves. Dillo was still feeling angry at her sisters. Then she spotted a movement under some leaves.

"Look, Marmma, I found one!" said Dillo with excitement as she pounced on the ground to capture the squiggly worm.

"Oh, Dillo, good for you," said Marmma. And they began eating the juicy worm together. Marmma chewed from one end of the worm and Dillo from the other end. Even though Lillo, Pillo, and Jillo were busy eating ants, they did notice that Marmma had helped Dillo find food.

"Marmma didn't help us," said Jillo between bites of ants.

"I know, and it isn't fair," said Pillo.

12

Randi T. Eddy

Lillo just nodded her head in agreement while her sticky tongue was searching her nose for pesky ants.

"Dillo's always the first to be fed, the first to be cleaned, and now the first to be taught how to use her nose to find worms," said Jillo.

"Yeah, and she never gets angry or sad. She just keeps smiling all the time. I think Dillo is Marmma's favorite," added Pillo.

"Yeah, me too," agreed Lillo. The three young armadillos continued to eat ants while thinking about why they didn't like Dillo.

Every morning after breakfast, Marmma would teach Dillo and her sisters about the environment in Bailey Tract. She taught them about the wet marsh, the plants, trees, and bushes. She especially taught them where to find the best food. They found worms, ants, beetles, and other insects by digging in the soft ground and under dead leaves. For special treats, they found crayfish and frogs and bird eggs in the grassy wetland. And sometimes they found dead things left over from a predator attack.

She taught them about the other animals in the refuge. "Some animals are friendly and some are not, especially alligators!" she would warn. "They will eat you any time of day."

Marmma always made sure Dillo was close to her when she gave her lessons. The sisters hated that Dillo got so much special attention.

13

- 2 -
The Sisters' Revenge

*O*ne night when the family was out foraging for food, the three sisters snuck away from Dillo and Marmma and met behind the roots of a large strangler fig tree that had been blown over by a tropical storm. They talked about how they could get rid of Dillo.

"Let's take her far away and get her lost," suggested Jillo.

"That's a great idea, Jillo, but where can we take her?" asked Lillo.

"I know," said Pillo, "we will take her to that forbidden pond that Marmma told us about. You know, where that big alligator lives."

"Oh, yeah," said Pillo, "then maybe the alligator will have her for dinner." And they all laughed with menacing delight.

"Wait a minute," said Lillo. "Do you know where the forbidden pond is?"

"I know where it is," said Pillo. "Remember that day I almost got lost near there?"

"Yeah, and Marmma found you and brought you home," said Jillo.

"But how are we going to find our way back home?" asked Lillo.

"We can leave a trail of scratch holes in the path. Then when we go home, we can cover them up so Dillo can't follow the trail," suggested Jillo.

"Good idea," agreed Lillo.

"And good riddance!" said Pillo.

"OK, it's set then. Tomorrow we say good-bye to Dillo," Jillo said.

The three girls tried to smile, but they couldn't.

The next morning, before the sun rose, the armadillo family was out looking for breakfast. Dillo loved to go out foraging with her family, even though her sisters were mean to her. She didn't understand why Pillo would snap a branch into her face, or Jillo would push her in a mud puddle, or Lillo would yank food right out of her mouth when Marmma wasn't looking.

Dillo managed to put up with her sisters' meanness because she loved being out with Marmma. She especially liked making new friends with the harmless animals in the Bailey Tract.

Dillo made friends easily since her smile made her very cute. She would just say "hi" to a snake slithering by, or a raccoon backing down the trunk of a palm tree. Noticing her smile, they would say "hi" back to her and go about their business.

When Lillo said "hi" to the snake, it would hiss at her and slither away. The raccoon would turn up her nose at Pillo and jog away from her. A yellow-crowned night heron would just ignore Jillo, pretending she wasn't there. The sisters resented Dillo's ability to make friends so easily, especially when they couldn't. Their patience was wearing thin. It was time to put their plan into action.

They found Dillo searching for food under the dead leaves of a wild lime tree. They looked around for Marmma and saw that she was busy digging for beetles far enough away that she couldn't hear them.

"Dillo," they called together.

Dillo looked up and smiled, only because she couldn't help it.

"Dillo, we know where there is a great place to eat with lots of snails and worms and beetles and spiders," said Pillo.

"Come with us, Dillo," Jillo said. "We'll show you where we all can have a feast."

Dillo didn't know why they were being so nice to her all of a sudden, but she was very hungry. She reluctantly decided to follow them.

They walked and walked. Finally, Dillo asked, "Won't we get lost going this far from Marmma, and what about the alligators?"

"Don't worry, Dillo, we know where we're going," said Pillo.

"And look here, Dillo," said Jillo, "I am making scratch marks on the trail so we can follow them back home."

Dillo thought that was a very smart thing to do, and relaxed a little.

"The feast is going to be great, Dillo," added Lillo.

"Why are you all being so nice to me?" asked Dillo.

"Oh, look, we are here!" exclaimed Jillo, not answering Dillo's question. They finally stopped at a place near the edge of a big pond.

"Oh, boy!" cheered Pillo and Lillo in unison.

"Look over there," said Jillo, pointing at some leather ferns and a salt bush. "Dig under the leaves and you'll find lots to eat."

Dillo looked at the salt bush and ferns. Still not trusting her sisters totally, she cautiously went over to the ferns. She was surprised and thrilled to find lots of beetles and worms. While chewing a scrumptious beetle, she looked up at her sisters and thought maybe they weren't so bad after all. "I wonder if they like me now, even with my smile," she thought.

The four sisters feasted on the abundant breakfast. After a while, Dillo realized that she was very full. She looked up to thank her sisters, but they were nowhere in sight. She looked all around. She called out "Hello," and heard nothing in return. **"Jillo? Pillo? Lillo? Where are you?"** she called.

She felt a little scared, but her smile wouldn't go away. Dillo had been so busy eating that she never noticed her three sisters had gone away and left her alone.

"Maybe they are in the bushes playing hide and seek," she thought.

Dillo searched around the area calling out for them, but she couldn't find them anywhere. Then she remembered that Jillo had made scratch marks on the trail. She searched all around for the marks. She looked in every direction, but there were no scratch marks to be found.

Dillo was very frightened. She didn't know where she was or how to get back home to Marmma. She sadly realized that her sisters weren't so nice after all. They had left her alone on purpose, just to be mean. She didn't know what to do. So she just sat in one spot, sad and alone, wishing her Marmma would find her. Tears began to flow down her little nose past her smiling mouth. She did look kind of silly as she sat crying with a smile that brightened up her face. She certainly didn't feel like smiling, but she couldn't help it.

"Marmma," she sobbed.

- 3 -
Marsha Rabbit

*T*hrough her sobbing, Dillo heard a noise in the tall spartina grass behind her. Her first thought was, "Marmma found me." But when she turned around, she didn't see a thing. Then she realized what it could be and shook with fear. **The alligator!**

She froze on the spot until she saw two long brown ears sticking up out of the grass. She knew alligators didn't have ears. She also knew it wasn't Marmma, because armadillo ears are cone-shaped, kind of pink, and not that long.

Dillo mustered up all the courage she could, and said, "Hello?"

A surprised small brown marsh rabbit looked up. She saw Dillo and thought, "Oh, it's only an armadillo." The rabbit went back to eating grass.

Marmma had taught Dillo about rabbits and knew they were harmless.

"Excuse me," Dillo sniffled. "Have you seen my three sisters?"

The rabbit raised her head again to take a closer look at Dillo.

"You are the only armadillo I've seen around here," the rabbit answered. "What are you doing out this time of day? The sun has come up and I thought armadillos go out only at night."

"My name is Dillo

17

and my sisters brought me here to eat breakfast. They have gone away and left me." Dillo began to sob again.

The rabbit felt sorry for the young armadillo, and then noticed the expression on Dillo's face.

"If you are lost, and so sad, why are you smiling?" the rabbit asked.

"I can't help it," Dillo whimpered. "I was born this way."

"How do you look when you are scared?" asked the rabbit.

"I don't know. I've never been scared—until now. I guess I look this way all the time," replied Dillo.

"That's the strangest thing I've ever seen," the rabbit chuckled.

Dillo felt terrible. She was scared and very sad, and all the rabbit could do was laugh at her. Dillo hated her smile.

"You are cute though, even if you are scared," the rabbit said. "My name is Marsha Rabbit."

"Nice to meet you, Marsha Rabbit," Dillo said, blinking the tears out of her eyes.

"Well, Dillo, you should be scared," said Marsha Rabbit. "Don't you know about the alligators in the marsh ponds?"

"Oh yes, I know about alligators," said Dillo. "But I've never seen one."

18

"Then you should know, Dillo, that alligators are big, long, greenish-black, sneaky, slithering, monster lizard-looking things, with a long mouth full of big sharp teeth that will grab you and pull you under the water to drown you. Then they eat you!"

Dillo shuddered at the thought. "Yes, Marmma taught us about them. She told us never to go near an alligator."

"Well, you better pray you never end up close to one, Dillo," warned Marsha Rabbit.

"But how do you know when one is near?" asked Dillo.

"Often you can see them sunning themselves on the sandy edge of the rivers and ponds. But when they are really hungry they go lurking underneath the water with just their eyes and the tip of their nose sticking up out of the surface. They look just like a log in the water. So sometimes an unfortunate heron or egret will land on them, and then – SNAP and GULP – no more bird."

"Oh dear," said Dillo. "I wouldn't ever want to stand on a log in the water."

"No, but you do get thirsty. And just drinking from the edge of the marsh pond could put you in danger," said Marsha Rabbit.

"Yeah, I'm thirsty now," admitted Dillo.

"Well, be careful where you drink because there is one huge alligator that lives in a big pond near here. His name is Snout, and he hunts for all kinds of living creatures. Snout will eat anything that comes close to his huge mouth, including you," warned Marsha Rabbit.

"If Snout is so bad, why are you here?" asked Dillo.

"We marsh rabbits are very smart, Dillo. We learn early in life how to tell the difference between a real log in the water and an alligator's head. Besides, we live in the thick bushes and underground in our warren, where the alligator can't go."

"Oh," said Dillo, remembering her home was also under the ground. "I just want to be home with my Marmma," she said with a whimper.

"I know who may have seen your sisters around here," said Marsha Rabbit. "Go down that sandy path next to the river," she said, pointing her little paw in the direction of the path. "You will come to another path that goes off to the left. That's where you might find Bob Cat and his family. Their home is in a deep hollow under a big tree near a shell mound not far from the path. I can't take you there because they will be tempted to eat me for lunch. I don't think they will eat you, Dillo, because you have hard plates on your back. Besides, when they see

19

your smile, I'm certain they will help you."

"OK, I'll try to find them---that is, if you are sure they won't eat me," said Dillo.

"You'll be fine, Dillo," assured Marsha Rabbit.

"Thanks for your help, Marsha Rabbit. I will never forget you," said Dillo, smiling at her for real.

"Good luck, Dillo, I hope you find your Marmma soon," Marsha Rabbit said, as she hopped under some leather ferns with her fluffy tail bobbing up and down.

Dillo was all alone again. She didn't know much about bobcats, only that Marmma had told her to stay away from them because they could be dangerous to baby armadillos. But Marsha Rabbit said they might be able to help her. "Maybe my smile will help," she thought. If that turned out to be true, then she would really be happy to have her smile. So she decided to be brave and try to find them. Marmma had taught her that being brave is good, but, at the same time, always to be aware of possible danger. "Don't be brave and foolish." Marmma would say. "Be brave and wise. You will live longer."

"I hope I can be brave and wise," Dillo thought as she took a big, deep breath and started to walk down the path where Marsha Rabbit had told her to go.

- 4 -
Bob Cat

Dillo walked and walked down the sandy path. She felt very sad as she thought of her mean sisters, who had left her lost and alone. One time when they were especially mean to her, Marmma had taught her that when she was sad or upset, she should try to think of more pleasant things. Then she might not feel so awful. So as she walked along, Dillo looked at all the different bushes, trees, grasses, ferns, and flowers. She decided to make a game of it and tried to name them all.

She saw a wax myrtle tree with tiny gray berries that birds love to eat. She said "hi" to a small gray catbird feasting on the berries. Then she saw a red-bellied woodpecker climbing up the side of a cabbage palm tree looking for ants and bugs. She wondered why it was called a "red-bellied" and not a "red-headed" woodpecker, since the top of its head was bright red. She did see a little red on its belly, so she decided the name was OK.

She saw a gumbo limbo tree with its peeling bark. And then, as if nature intended to spread color about, she saw some morning glories with big beautiful purple flowers. It made her feel good just to look at those blossoms. Then she walked by a salt bush that Marmma said blooms in the fall with white feathery seeds that fly in the wind and tickles your nose. "Snow tickles your nose, too," Marmma had told her. She wondered why it was called a salt bush and not a snow bush. She thought that someday she would like to see snow. She would have to ask Marmma lots of questions when she was with her again. "Marmma always teaches me a lot," she thought.

The Name-It game was kind of fun, but Dillo was becoming tired and thirsty. She turned to go to the river for a drink. Then she remembered Marsha Rabbit's warning about alligators, especially Snout, and decided she would try to do without water for a little while longer. She kept walking on the edge of the path. The sun was becoming very hot on her back, even though her plates protected her from sunburn. She really wanted to take a nap, but she was determined to get home and find Marmma, no matter what she had to endure.

Continuing to walk, Dillo saw a beautiful black and white striped zebra longwing butterfly eating the nectar from a flower of a Spanish needle plant. She stopped on the path and said "hi" to the butterfly. The butterfly fluttered down right onto the tip of her nose. Dillo thought it was giving her a kiss. It slowly flapped its wings several times as Dillo looked cross-eyed at the butterfly on her nose. She stood very still and just smiled. Then the butterfly flew away to another tasty flower.

"That was neat," Dillo said out loud, and continued walking down the path.

After a big yawn, Dillo realized that she was very tired. She spotted a small burrow under a big log at the side of the path, and went over to it. She sniffed inside. "Hello," she called. She went farther into the hole in the ground and found no one there. "I'll just take a little nap," she thought to herself. She curled up and fell instantly to sleep.

Dillo awoke suddenly when she heard a rustling noise outside of the burrow. Her little heart raced with fear, and she didn't move a muscle. She didn't hear anything for a while, so she quietly crawled up to the entrance of the burrow. She peered out and could see that nothing was there. But then she heard more rustling in the spartina grass just beyond the log. She couldn't decide whether to make a run for it or stay in the burrow. Suddenly, before she could do anything, a big brownish furry spotted animal with a stubby tail came out of the grass. It turned its head to look at her. They just stared at each other. The animal sniffed at the air toward Dillo. Dillo froze with fear, thinking her life was about to end.

Then the animal said, "Hi, I'm Bob Cat. I haven't seen you around here before."

"Bob Cat, hello!" Dillo said with great relief. "My name is Dillo. Marsha Rabbit told me to try to find you. She said you might be able to help me find my way home."

Dillo came out of the burrow and proceeded to tell Bob Cat the

Rauder T. Eddy

story of her sisters leaving her by the pond, all alone. She finished by saying that she was lost and thirsty and wanted to go home.

"That is a very sad story, Dillo," Bob Cat said. "I haven't seen your sisters and I have no idea where your home is."

"Oh," Dillo said sadly, and put her head down.

Then Bob Cat said, "Why don't you follow me to my home, Dillo? We would love to have you for dinner."

"NO," Dillo said, quickly backing up in fear.

Then Bob Cat said with a chuckle, "Oh, Dillo, I don't mean we are going to **eat** you for dinner, we want you to join us for dinner. We don't usually eat armadillos. The plates around your back are too hard for us to bite through," said Bob Cat, still laughing. "Besides, we much prefer eating delicious, big, juicy rabbits and birds."

"Poor Marsha Rabbit," thought Dillo.

"I wasn't sure," said Dillo. "I've never been alone before, and I'm scared."

"Dillo, if you're so scared, why are you smiling?" asked Bob Cat.

"Here we go again," Dillo thought. "I was born this way and I smile whether I like it or not," she said. "I am not smiling inside, but you would never know it. Even when I want to look mean and show my teeth, everyone laughs at me because they think it's just a big grin."

"That must be very frustrating," said Bob Cat. "But you are cute with that smile."

"Thanks," said Dillo softly, not really caring if

23

she was cute or not.

"Come on, Dillo, let's head for home," Bob Cat said, turning to go off the path. Dillo followed Bob Cat through a lot of saw grass and leather ferns, until they came to an opening onto another sandy path that ran beside a river. It was getting late in the day and Dillo was very tired. Even though it was March and warm during the day, the nights were still quite cool. It was already in the low 50s, and Dillo began to shiver in spite of the protective plates on her back.

"Are you all right, Dillo?" asked Bob Cat.

"Yes, but I'm cold," said Dillo, shivering. "I am used to snuggling up with Marmma when it's cold."

"We are almost to our den. After dinner, you can spend the night with us. With all our warm coats, you should be as snug as an opossum baby in its mother's pouch. But first let's have a drink from the river. I will look out for alligators while you drink," offered Bob Cat.

"Thanks, Bob Cat," said Dillo gratefully.

They walked cautiously down the bank of the river to the water. Bob Cat looked from side to side for any signs of danger. He raised his head and smelled in the wind for alligators.

"It's OK, Dillo, go ahead and drink."

Dillo slowly approached the water's edge, and just as she put her mouth into the water, there was a big splash right in the middle of the river.

"*AAHHHHHHH*," shouted Dillo, running back up the bank.

"Oh, it's all right, Dillo. That was just an osprey swooping in to catch a fish in the water. They do it all the time," said Bob Cat, trying to calm down the frightened little armadillo.

They both watched the osprey fly away with a long squirming fish in its talons. Then Dillo tiptoed down the slope again to the water's edge. She drank and drank until she thought she was going to burst. Bob Cat drank too, and finally said, "OK Dillo, let's get home."

When they started to walk again, Dillo thought of her home.

"I miss my Marmma," Dillo said, thinking out loud.

"Tomorrow we will try to find out where you live, Dillo," said Bob Cat.

Feeling exhausted, Dillo whispered, "OK."

Walking half asleep, Dillo heard Bob Cat say, "We're home, Dillo."

Dillo looked and saw an opening in the ground underneath an old gumbo limbo tree stump surrounded by bushes. Suddenly another bobcat emerged from the hollow, and Dillo jumped back. It touched noses with Bob Cat's and then looked at Dillo, sniffing the air.

"Dillo, this is Bea Cat, the mother of our kittens. Bea, this is Dillo. Dillo is lost. I invited her to have dinner and to sleep with us for the night," explained Bob Cat.

"Hello, Dillo, what a nice smile you have," said Bea kindly. "Welcome to our home."

"Thank you for being so nice to me," said Dillo, as her attention turned to a scurry of movement at the den opening. She watched three very small bobcat kittens emerge from the hole in the ground. They smelled all around and then ran right up to Dillo. They smelled her all over her body.

"They won't hurt you, Dillo," assured Bea Cat. "They are just curious and happy to have a new friend come and visit."

"Ouch!" *said Dillo, startled, as one of the kittens attacked her tail.*

"Kits! Let go of Dillo's tail. She is our guest for the night and you will be nice to her," scolded Bea Cat.

"Let's eat," said Bob Cat, dragging the smelly half-eaten carcass of a raccoon from under a bush, where it was hidden. The baby bobcats pounced on the dead animal and tore at its flesh.

"Help yourself, Dillo. We found it on the road where a big, fast, noisy thing rolled over it," offered Bea Cat.

"Thanks, but I'd rather look for a few worms and ants," said Dillo.

So while the bobcats devoured the remains of the raccoon, Dillo did find a few morsels of insects for herself under some dead leaves below a strangler fig tree.

When dinner was finished, Bob Cat instructed, "OK everyone, let's get out of the cold and go to sleep for a while. Later, when it's really dark tonight, we'll go hunting for breakfast."

So they all went into the den and snuggled together. The adult bobcats and kittens surrounded Dillo, making her feel nice and warm. To Dillo, it was almost like being back home safely in Marmma's arms. She dozed off into a sound sleep.

Early the next morning Dillo was startled awake by a sharp pain in one of her ears.

"*OWWW!*" she yelled as one of the kittens was biting her ear while playing "Catch the Mouse" with it. She emerged out of the den with the kittens painfully attached to her ear and tail. After shaking them off, she looked around and saw the light of the rising sun beaming against the orange and purple sky. As she stretched her sleepy body, one of the kittens attacked her ear again.

"Where are your parents?" she asked, brushing the little bobcat off her head.

One of the kittens licked her whiskers, indicating that they were out getting food for them.

Just then, Bea Cat arrived with Bob Cat right behind her. Bob Cat had a brown furry thing with long ears hanging from his mouth.

"Breakfast!" Bea Cat announced.

Bob Cat dropped the dead rabbit on the ground in front of her. Dillo froze where she was standing. "OH, NO! Marsha, my friend," she cried.

They all looked at each other and then at the dead rabbit.

"No, no, Dillo, don't worry," assured Bob Cat. "This is not your friend Marsha Rabbit. This is a male rabbit we found near the river."

Dillo was very relieved that it wasn't Marsha Rabbit as she watched the kittens pounce on the dead animal, creating a storm of flying fur.

"I am sorry this upsets you, Dillo," said Bea Cat. "You have to understand that we bobcats do eat meat."

"I know," said Dillo. "Marsha Rabbit was so kind to me. I wouldn't want anything to happen to her."

"We know Marsha Rabbit, Dillo, and since she is your friend, we won't do anything to harm her," said Bob Cat.

"Besides, she is very good at hiding from predators," added Bea Cat.

One of the kittens decided that Dillo's tail was much more interesting than tasteless fur, and pounced on it with claws and teeth.

"**OUCH!**" cried Dillo again, and the kitten let go.

Dillo looked pleadingly at them and said, "I just want to go home now. Can you help me?"

"I don't know where your home is, Dillo, but I do know someone who might be able to help you get there," said Bob Cat, sympathizing with Dillo's predicament. "Come with me."

"Good luck, Dillo," called Bea Cat as she watched her walk away from the den, following Bob Cat.

"Thanks for the warm night, Bea Cat," Dillo called back. "Bye, kits," she said, very glad to be away from those pesky kittens.

Dillo followed Bob Cat through the bushes.

Rauder T. Eddy

27

- 5 -

Oliver Owl

*B*ob Cat led Dillo to a shady stand of buttonwood trees. All of a sudden Bob Cat stopped, took a deep breath, raised his head, and yowled like a cat and a lion combined.

"AARRRROOOOWWWWWWWWWWWWWOoooooooo."

Dillo looked at him in amazement. Then it became so quiet you could hear a leaf drop. Off in the distance they could hear a faint "Hoo, Hoo, Hooooooooooo."

Bob Cat made his crying sound again, this time not so loud and long. "ARRROOOWWWWWWWWWWOooo."

"Hooo, Hoooooooo" was heard again, only this time closer to them.

"Here comes my friend Oliver, the great horned owl," said Bob Cat. "He saved my life when I was a kitten. You see, when I was about five weeks old, I was drinking from the river with my Mama Cat when a huge osprey swooped down and grabbed me in its talons. It must have thought I was a fish, because a mullet jumped right next to me and the osprey got me instead. It started to fly up above the trees and saw that I wasn't a fish at all. Ospreys' favorite food is fish, you know. So, miraculously, it just let go and I dropped down right into a big bird's nest in a strangler fig tree. It was Oliver and Olive Owl's nest. I was a bloody mess from the osprey's talons, and they took pity on me. After a while Oliver took me gently in his talons and flew me back home to my den, where my Mama Cat licked my wounds. Oliver knew where I lived because he is very wise and knows everything that goes on in the Bailey Tract," Bob Cat explained.

"HELLOOOO," a voice said from above.

They both looked up and there, perched on a branch of a buttonwood tree, staring down at them, was a very large brown bird with big yellow eyes, stand-up feathered ears, and a black curved bill.

"Wow," said Dillo, looking up at the huge bird.

"Oliver!" called Bob Cat. "This is Dillo, my new friend. She's lost and wants to go home to her Marmma. We thought maybe you could help."

The owl flew down to the ground and stood towering over Dillo. "Hellooo, Dillooo," said Oliver in a soft hooting voice.

Dillo looked up in wonderment at Oliver's big yellow eyes and said, "Hello, Oliver."

Bob Cat proceeded to tell Oliver the story of Dillo's three scheming sisters leaving her lost and alone.

When he was finished, Oliver said, "Hoo hoooo, that is a woooful tale, Dillooo."

"Can you help me get home?" Dillo asked Oliver. "I just want to go home and be with my Marmma," she said, trying to control a sob.

"I might be able to help you, Dilloooo, but first answer a question for me. If you are so sad, why are you smiling?"

"She can't help it," offered Bob Cat. "She was born that way and can't stop smiling."

"Oohoooo. Then no one knows when you are sad, or mad, or afraid?" asked Oliver.

"No, and when I tell them I am sad, or mad, they don't believe me and just laugh at me," said Dillo.

"Ohooooooo," said Oliver, shaking his head back and forth.

"Well, Dillo," interrupted Bob Cat, "I must get home to my family. I hope you find your way home soon."

"Good-bye, Bob Cat, thanks for all your help. I will never forget you," said Dillo.

"Bye Dillo, bye Oliver," said Bob Cat, and he loped away.

Then Oliver asked, "Dillooo, would you like to be able to express yourself better? Would you like it if others could see that you are afraid, or mad, or even sad?"

"Oh, yes, Oliver, but I can't with this smile," said Dillo.

"Well, before I send you on your way home, I will teach you how to use your body to express yourself," said Oliver.

And Oliver began to help Dillo do just that.

"Now, Dillooo, when you are happy, point your tail up toward the sun, hold your head high, and show your nice smile."

Dillo had no problem smiling, of course, or holding her head high. But pointing her tail straight up in the air was a bit difficult, since the plates on her back held it down.

"I can't point my tail up, Oliver," said Dillo.

"Ummmm, can you curl your tail so the tip points upward?" asked Oliver.

"How's this?" asked Dillo, curling her tail as best she could.

"Good, Dillooo. That will do just fine," Oliver said. "Now," he continued, "when you are afraid, or in danger, tuck your tail under your back legs, put your head down between your front legs, and bring all your legs in under your belly. You will look like a little barrel."

Dillo tried to put her long tail under her by straightening her back legs as tall as she could and forcing her tail between them. But that tail just wouldn't bend under her.

"OK, Dillo, try lifting one of your back legs, and whip your tail under the leg," suggested Oliver.

Dillo lifted her left back leg up, stood tall on the other three legs, and whipped her tail under herself so hard that she lost her balance and fell over onto her side. Without even thinking, to protect herself, she tucked in her legs and her head, and rolled over several times like a barrel.

"That's great, Dillooo!" Oliver said. "Now hold that position."

Oliver went over to Dillo, still rolled up, and pushed her hard with his sharp talons. She just rolled and rolled, until a clump of grass stopped her.

"See, Dillooo?" said Oliver. "That doesn't hurt at all, and you are fully protected."

Dillo stretched her body out and said, "Wow, Oliver, that really works."

"You learn very fast, Dillooo. Now comes the hard part. When you are angry, slap your tail on the ground three times."

Dillo did so, and yelled, "OOOWWWWOOO!" She had slapped her tail on a rock.

"OH, HO, HOOOOO," laughed Oliver. "Try to slap your tail on softer ground next time, Dilloooo," he said, still laughing.

Dillo checked the ground behind her and slapped her tail three times on soft sandy ground.

"That's very good, Dillooo, but you might also put your nose to the ground and bare your teeth when you slap your tail, so you look more fierce."

Dillo put her head down, lifted her lips, showed her teeth, and slapped her tail on the ground as Oliver had instructed her to do.

"That's great, Dillooo," Oliver said. "Now add one more thing. Growl as loud as you can."

"Growl?" asked Dillo. "Armadillos don't growl, Oliver."

"Well, pretend you are a big, fierce animal and make the loudest, meanest noise you can," suggested Oliver.

Dillo remembered how Bob Cat roared, and that was very scary, even if he was only calling for Oliver. So she started with her nose on the ground, bared her teeth, started with "GGGRRR," then brought her head up high, opened her mouth, showed all her teeth, and let loose with a "GGGRRROOOOOOOOWWWWWWWWWOOOO."

31

"That will do just fine, Dillooo," said Oliver, chuckling at Dillo's little voice. "And don't forget to slap your tail while you are growling."

"OK, Oliver, I will. But what if I am sad, Oliver? What can I do then?" asked Dillo.

"Hummmmm," thought Oliver. "Put your head down and your front feet on your face so you are hiding your smile, and then sniffle."

Dillo put her feet on her face, and then she went "sniff, sniff, sniff," which was followed by great coughing and sneezing from sand that had gone up her nose during her sniffling.

Oliver laughed and laughed. "OOH, HO, HO, HOOOOO!" Then he said, "One more thing, Dillooo, when you sniff, be careful where you put your nose, oh, ho, ho, hooo."

Dillo tried it again, this time being careful not to inhale any dirt or sand.

"Sniff, sniff, sniff." Then she looked up at Oliver with her smiling face.

"Perfect, Dillooo!" Oliver exclaimed. "Now let's go and test it all."

"Test it?" asked Dillo.

"Yes," said Oliver.

"Follow me, Dillooo."

And off they went.

Gogo Gopher Tortoise

*O*liver flew off through the trees and onto a sandy path. Dillo ran as fast as her little legs would go to catch up with Oliver. Breathing very hard, she finally caught up to him.

"This looks like a good place," said Oliver. Then he flew up onto a branch of a gumbo limbo tree, where he could watch Dillo try out her new expressions.

"OK Dillooo," said Oliver softly. "It won't be long before someone comes along."

"What do I do when they get here?" asked Dillo.

"Do whatever you feel like doing, Dillooo. Just pretend you are alone and I am not here," whispered Oliver.

Dillo sat and waited in the shade of a leather fern. With nothing to do, she thought of Marmma and how much she missed her. A great feeling of sadness and homesickness welled up inside her. She put her head down and her front feet over her face. She began sniffling and forgot all about Oliver watching her. She just felt like crying. She couldn't help it. She just missed her Marmma so much.

"Are you OK?" asked a slow, deep-sounding voice.

Dillo looked up with tears rolling down her face. She saw a big brown mound with four legs and a head slowly plodding toward her. Whatever it was didn't seem to be threatening at all.

"Who are you?" asked Dillo, with a sniffle.

"I'm Gogo Gopher Tortoise. Who are you?"

"I'm Dillo Armadillo," said Dillo, standing up and looking at Gogo.

"You looked very sad when I first saw you, Dillo, but now I see you are smiling. Are you sad or happy?" asked Gogo.

"Hellooooo Gogoooo," Oliver called from above, interrupting the conversation.

Looking up, Gogo said, "Oh, hi Oliver. What are you doing up there?"

"My friend Dillooo is learning how to express her feelings. See, Dillooo, it worked!" exclaimed Oliver as he flew down to the path.

"Gogooo thought you were sad when he first saw you."

"I was, and I still am," said Dillo. "I guess you were right, Oliver, it does help to hide my smile."

"What are you two talking about? Why would anyone want to hide their smile?" asked Gogo, in his slow, deep voice.

"You never really know what is underneath a smile, Gogooo," said Oliver, flying down to the ground next to Dillo. "Dillooo is my new friend, and . . ." Oliver proceeded to tell Gogo all about Dillo and her tale of woe.

When he finished, Gogo looked at Dillo and said, "Wow, Dillo, I have never heard such a story in my life. Is there anything I can do to help you?"

"Oliver is helping me, but thanks for the offer, Gogo."

"So, how are you today, Gogooo?" Oliver asked.

"The same as most days, Oliver, except when I came out of my hole in the ground this morning, that yellow Whipper Rat Snake was waiting for me. He was up to his old nasty tricks and scared me almost to death," explained Gogo.

"Who is Whipper Rat Snake?" asked Dillo, looking up, suddenly curious.

"Whipper Rat is a mean yellow rat snake who delights in scaring anyone who comes within smelling distance of his nasty forked tongue," said Oliver.

"Yeah, without warning, he slithers out right in front of you, coils up, and spits out 'HISSSSSSSSSSS' with his mouth wide open. Then he unwinds and whips his tail around right in your face, laughs out loud, and slithers away. It is very annoying," said Gogo.

"Most rat snakes are usually harmless, Dillooo, except to mice and other small animals," said Oliver. "They especially like to slither up into trees and eat birds and eggs and lizards. This rat snake got his name, 'Whipper,' one day when he was eating eggs in a red-shouldered hawk's nest. The mother hawk attacked him and stuck her sharp bill into his side. He whipped his tail around so hard that it snapped like a whip in her face and she let go of him. He dropped to the ground and has been a mean bully ever since."

"Yeah," said Gogo. "That's the way life is sometimes. Once in a while, living creatures will become mean and nasty when they have been treated in mean and nasty ways."

"What about my sisters?" asked Dillo. "They have been treated with love and care by my Marmma, so why are they so mean to me?"

"Maybe they are jealous of the attention your Marmma gives you, Dillooo," suggested Oliver. "Jealousy is another feeling that can make creatures behave in unpleasant ways. Anyway, it's time someone stood up to that Whipper Rat Snake," he said, looking right at Dillo.

Then Gogo looked at Dillo.

"OH NOOO, not me, Oliver," insisted Dillo, knowing exactly what Oliver was going to ask her to do.

"You can do it, Dillooo," encouraged Oliver. "Show Gogo your mad and mean act. See what he thinks."

"Dillo, I can't believe you could look mean or mad with that smile on your face," challenged Gogo.

Dillo took the challenge. She put her head down, showed her teeth, lifted her head up, growled "GGGRRRRRROOOOWWW" as loud as she thought she could, and slapped her tail so hard against the ground that sand and dust came up and covered them both.

Oliver roared with laughter. "AHHH-HAHAHA-HOHOHO. That's great, Dillooooo!" he exclaimed, shaking the dust off his feathers.

"WOW, Dillo, I really was scared for a minute," said Gogo in amazement.

"Thanks," said Dillo, smiling on purpose and very proud of her new achievement.

"OK, now let's try it out on Whipper Rat Snake. Come on, Dillooo," said Oliver, flying up the path where Gogo had come from.

"I don't know," said Dillo, with an uncertain tone. She really didn't think she could stand up to a real enemy.

"You can do it, Dillo," encouraged Gogo. "Be brave, and good luck!"

- 7 -

Whipper Rat Snake

*D*illo reluctantly followed Oliver up the path, becoming more worried with every step. She did not like the idea of being whipped in the face with a rat snake's tail.

"Youuuu can dooooo it Dilloooooo," she heard Oliver hoot from above.

They kept going farther up the path. Dillo began to think, with relief, that the snake was no longer around. But suddenly, without warning, Whipper Rat Snake slithered out from between two clumps of spartina grass right in front of Dillo and spat out "HISSSSSSSSSSSSSS," with his mouth wide open. Then he slithered around Dillo and, without warning, whipped his tail right into Dillo's nose.

"**OWWWWW!**" cried Dillo, in pain. She started to bury her head in her hands and roll up into a ball. But then she heard "DILLOOOOOO" from above, while Whipper Rat Snake laughed and slithered around her, getting ready to coil up and whip her again.

"**I can't let Oliver down,**" she thought to herself. "Be strong, remember what Oliver taught you."

In an instant, with all the courage she could muster, she stood as tall as her little legs would allow, put her head down, showed her teeth, and roared the loudest growl she could manage while lifting her head up high. "**GGGGRRRROOOOOOOOOOOWWWWWWWWWWOOoooo.**"

Whipper Rat Snake stopped slithering and stared at Dillo in amazement as she slapped her tail on the path as hard as she could. A cloud of dirt and sand rose into the air above them. Whipper then decided he wanted nothing to do with this crazy little armadillo, so he turned away from Dillo and swiftly slithered away.

"**BRAVOOOOOOOOOOOOOO!**" hooted Oliver from above.

"Way to go, Dillo!" said Gogo, just arriving from down the path. "I just had to see you put that Whipper Rat Snake in his place, Dillo, and you did!"

"Gee, I guess I did," said Dillo, shaking the sand from her back.

"Well, Dillooo," said Oliver, "I think you are ready to find your way home without any problem from bullies. The only danger you have to watch out for is Snout. He is an ugly, huge alligator who lives in the big pond at the end of the Bailey Tract. Humans call it Smith Pond, but we call it Snout Pond."

"Snout has been known to travel great distances and eat anything that moves, including stray dogs and cats who wander away from their homes," added Gogo.

"Yes, I've heard about alligators. They were the first thing Marmma warned us about when we started to go out on our own," said Dillo.

"OK, Dillooo, just follow this path by the river until you get to a turn to the left. You will see a wooden bridge that goes up and over the wet marshes. Go over that bridge and take another left. Go down that path past the first pond. That is Ani Pond. It will be on your right. After the pond the trail curves to the right. You will see more water on your left. Go over a small wooden bridge, and soon you will come to another sandy path. Turn left onto that path."

"Wow, Oliver, I don't think I can remember all that," said Dillo.

"OK, it's easy. Go left, over a big bridge, left, over a little bridge, then left onto a sandy path," said Oliver.

"I think I have it. Left, bridge, left, bridge, and left down a path," said Dillo.

"That's right, Dillooo," said Oliver.

"When do I take a right?" asked Dillo.

"Nooo, nooo, Dillooo, you don't take a right at all. I meant, **correct**. You were correct not to go right," said Oliver, laughing with delight.

"Oh," said Dillo, a little embarrassed.

"Now, after you make your last left, you will see a big pond on your left with a red mangrove island in the middle. Just beyond that pond, in the woods on the right, is where I think your home is," said Oliver.

"Have you been to my home, Oliver?" Dillo asked.

"Not exactly, Dillooo, but I have seen some big armadillos in that area, and one of them could be your Marmma."

"Oh, I hope so, Oliver," said Dillo.

"I imagine your Marmma will be looking for you, Dillooo, so you shouldn't have any trouble finding her."

"I can't wait to see her," said Dillo.

"Now Dillooo," warned Oliver, "if you go as far as the bench at the end of the path, STOP! The path there goes left and leads directly to Snout Pond!"

"I wouldn't want to go there," said Dillo. "OK, I think I know where to go now."

"If you get lost, just ask any bird where the Red Mangrove Pond is. The birds in Bailey Tract often look for fish in that pond," said Oliver.

"OK, Oliver," said Dillo.

"Well, Dillooo, I'd better get back to my nest before my family thinks I have abandoned them," said Oliver.

"Thanks for all your help, Oliver. I hope I will see you again. And you too, Gogo. I will miss you both," said Dillo.

"Good luck, Dillooo, I'm sure we will meet again," called Oliver.

"Safe journey, Dillo. Be sure to watch for alligators, especially Snout," added Gogo.

Dillo smiled and said, "Byeee." Then she stood up as tall as she could, pointed the tip of her tail up to the sky, and said, "I won't ever forget what you taught me."

Oliver waved the tip of his wing, and Gogo shook his head up and down. Then Dillo continued her journey up the path. There were times when she thought she really did feel like smiling.

- 8 -

Annie and Arnie Anhinga

After Dillo left Oliver and Gogo, she felt very excited about finally seeing Marmma again. She even felt quite brave after all the new things she had learned from Oliver. She picked up her pace and trotted up the path.

It wasn't long before Dillo realized she was very hungry. She looked around and found a big anthill just off the path in some short grass. With one swipe of her paw through the gray, sandy mound, the ants scrambled out to find what had attacked their nest. Dillo stuck her sticky tongue into the middle of hundreds of frenzied red fire ants and gulped them into her mouth. "Yummy," she said to herself. They were very sweet-tasting and she ate them like candy. She didn't mind that they were scrambling all over her body, trying to bite her. They had a nasty, painful sting, but not for Dillo. Her tough, leathery skin and hard plates kept the ants from stinging her. When she was full, she shook off the ants still trying to bite her, and continued down the path.

Then she came to the big wooden bridge that passed over the wet marsh. She started to walk over the bridge, but her little legs kept getting caught in between the boards.

"Ouch!" she yelled out loud. She stopped and looked how far she had to go to get across the bridge to the other end.

"Hummm, how am I going to get over this bridge?" she asked herself. "I know, I'll do it the way Marsha Rabbit would do it."

So she put all four feet on one board and tried to hop over the board in front of her onto the next one. It worked! HOP again, HOP, HOP, HOP, until her hopping took her all the way across the bridge. By the time she made it to the other end of the bridge, she was so tuckered out she could hardly breathe.

"Phew, that was really hard," she thought. Dillo sat down to rest for a minute. She heard a loud noise coming from above her. She looked up and saw a red-bellied woodpecker looking down at her, laughing his head off.

"What are you laughing at?" she asked the noisy woodpecker.

"I never saw an armadillo hop like a rabbit before, and you looked really funny," he said, continuing to laugh.

Dillo was irritated at being laughed at but was too tired to argue with a bird. "Never mind that, do you know where Ani Pond is?" she asked the bird.

"Right down that path," the bird said, and flew away, still laughing.

Dillo looked down the path that went to the left. "Left," she remembered Oliver saying. "That must be the way," she said to herself and continued walking.

She noticed a pond to her right. "Hum, that must be Ani Pond," she thought.

Dillo was very thirsty after her strenuous trip over the bridge, and the water in Ani Pond looked very good. She spotted a small opening between some leather ferns and snuck quietly between them down to the water's edge. She searched the pond's surface for anything that looked like a log just sticking up out of the water. Then she spotted two large black birds perched like statues on a branch by the shore of the pond. One bird had its wings spread straight out and its head pointing up toward the sky. She thought it looked quite beautiful in the sun with its shiny black and white wing feathers and long thin neck. The other bird appeared to be on the lookout, maybe for Snout. Both birds turned their heads toward Dillo when they heard her in the ferns.

Dillo wasn't sure if she should talk to these strange birds, but decided it was OK since Marmma had told her that most birds were harmless.

"Hello," she said. "My name is Dillo."

"Hello Dillo, I'm Annie Anhinga," said the bird, with her wings out straight, moving only her head. "This is my son, Arnie."

"Hi," said Arnie.

"Why are you standing there with your wings spread out like that?" asked Dillo.

"Because after we have been swimming for fish, our wings are wet and we can't fly. This is how we dry out," answered Annie.

"What are you doing out here in the daylight?" Arnie asked. "I thought armadillos sleep during the day."

"Oh, yeah, we usually do. But I'm lost and looking for my way back home." Then Dillo told Annie and Arnie her story.

When Dillo finished her story, Arnie said, "Your sisters must be really mean to leave you in the marsh, where Snout could get you."

Dillo put her head down with the thought of her sisters.

"You do look cute with your smile, though. I bet you make friends much easier than your sisters," added Annie, trying to cheer up Dillo.

"Yeah, I guess I do," replied Dillo, remembering her friends, Marsha, and Bea and Bob Cat, and Oliver, and Gogo. "But not everyone wants to be a friend," she said. Then she told Annie and Arnie about that yellow Whipper Rat Snake.

"Yeah, I know Whipper Rat Snake," said Annie. "He scared me once too. But I wasn't going to let him get away with it. So one day, when he was sunning himself on the sand near the edge of the pond, I swam in the water toward him. He looked at me and thought I was a snake too."

Arnie interrupted Annie's story and said, "You know, Dillo, that we are sometimes called the 'snakebird' because when we swim with our long dark necks gliding above the water's surface, we look like a snake in the water."

"Arnie, I am telling this story!" his mother scolded. "Anyway, Whipper Rat Snake doesn't mind other snakes, and he let me get close enough to him so that I, quick as a woodpecker, poked a hole in his side with my needle-sharp bill. Well, after I poked him, he let out a **'HISSSSSSSSSSSSSSS'** louder than I have ever heard a snake hiss. He whipped his tail all around, not knowing what hit him, and then took off like a scared rabbit."

Dillo laughed out loud. "Annie, what a great story. That Whipper Rat Snake deserved to be poked."

"Well, I guess it worked, because he hasn't bothered us since."
Taking a deep breath, Dillo asked, "Have you ever seen Snout?"

"Oh, yes, we have seen Snout, haven't we, Arnie?" Annie said sadly, and continued her story. "One day, after fishing, Arnie, my daughter Amy, and I were drying our wings on a branch by the water. All of a sudden, Snout exploded out of the water and grabbed Amy. He took her under the water and we never saw her again."

"How awful!" said Dillo.

"You be careful, Dillo," warned Annie. "Snout is very sneaky and can attack from anywhere, even on the sandy path."

"I know, I've been warned," said Dillo. "Is it safe to drink some water here, Annie?"

"Yes, go ahead and drink, Dillo. I'll keep a lookout for any movement in the water," said Annie.

Dillo took a long drink of water.

"Thanks for your help, Annie, and you too, Arnie. I have to go now. Nice meeting you both," said Dillo.

"It's nice to meet you too, Dillo. Good luck getting home," said Annie, still standing like a statue.

Dillo continued on her way. The path curved to the right and then she saw more water on her left. It looked like another river.

- 9 -
Eddy Egret

"*I* don't remember Oliver telling me about a river," Dillo said to herself as she walked down the path. She began to think she was lost again. She went over toward the river and saw a small muddy embankment going down to the water's edge. Then she spotted a worm squirming in the mud. She couldn't resist, so she quickly ran over and jumped on the worm in the mud. The mud was so slippery that she slid all the way down the embankment and almost into the water.

"Wow," she said, relieved she hadn't gone into the water. She also realized she still had the worm hanging out of her mouth. She stood up and finished eating her delicious snack. Then she saw a very large white bird with a long neck and a yellow bill standing on the other side of the water. Its head was moving in slow motion, while staring down into the water.

"Helloo," called Dillo, after swallowing the last of the worm.

The great egret looked up at Dillo and replied, "Be quiet! Can't you see I'm fishing?"

"Oh, I'm sorry to bother you. But I wonder if you could tell me where the Red Mangrove Pond is?" asked Dillo.

44

"You see, I'm lost and trying to find my way home. Oliver Owl told me to go past the Red Mangrove Pond."

"Oliver!" said the egret, not quite so irritated. "He is a good friend of mine. Any friend of Oliver's is a friend of mine. My name is Eddy. What's your name, little one?"

"My name is Dillo Armadillo," answered Dillo.

"You sure are a cute little armadillo. I like the way you smile. How did you get lost?"

And so Dillo told her whole story to the big white egret.

"That's quite a sad tale, Dillo. I haven't seen your sisters or your Marmma around here, but the Red Mangrove Pond is up the path, just past the little bridge," the egret said, pointing his bill in the direction of the bridge.

"Oh, good, and thanks," said Dillo, looking in the direction of the little bridge.

Dillo needed to drink some more water after eating the worm and asked, "Have you seen any alligators around here?"

"No, I haven't, but I got here just before you did," answered Eddy.

"I need a drink of water. Could you please watch for alligators?" asked Dillo.

"Sure thing, Dillo," said Eddy.

Dillo started to drink as Eddy took two long slow steps on the shoreline, searching the dark water for tasty minnows.

Suddenly there was a big splash in the water in front of Dillo. Then something burst out of the water right next to her.

"**AHHHHH,**" screamed Dillo as she jumped three feet in the air, landed, and instantly went into her "ball" position, fearing for her life.

"It's OK, Dillo," called Eddy Egret. "They are friends of mine."

- 10 -
Oozie and Ozzy Otter

*D*illo dared to peak out between her front feet and saw two very wet, brown, furry creatures she had never seen before. They shook the water off their fur and looked curiously at Dillo.

"Hi ya! My name is Ozzy Otter and this is my brother, Oozie Otter. Who are you?" Ozzy asked cheerfully.

"Oh, my name is Dillo Armadillo," she said with relief as she uncurled herself and stretched out.

"Dillo is lost and trying to find her way home," said Eddy. "Has either of you seen any armadillos in the area lately?"

"Nope," replied Ozzy. "Have you, Oozie?"

"No, I haven't seen any armadillos, but we did see Snout up to no good near the big pond at the end of the path," he said.

"You be careful, Dillo, Snout will eat anything," warned Ozzy.

"I know. Everyone has been telling me all about Snout," said Dillo.

"Hey, Dillo, you look like a happy sort, smiling and all. Do you want

to play slide with us?" asked Oozie

"Just because I look like I'm smiling, doesn't mean I'm happy. I am not happy! I'm homesick, and I just want to find my Marmma," said Dillo, lowering her head to the ground.

"Well, maybe playing slide will cheer you up," said Ozzy cheerfully.

"I don't know how to play slide," said Dillo, really wanting to get on her way.

"Watch," said Ozzy.

The two otters climbed up the slippery slope and stood looking down the muddy chute. Ozzy went first. He lay flat on his tummy, pushed forward with all four feet, and began to slide, keeping his feet up off the mud.

"**WHEEEEEEEEE,**" he yelled with glee, as he slid down the slope head first into the water.

Then "**WHEEEEEEEEE,**" yelled Oozie, as he slid down and splashed into the water next to Ozzy.

They both climbed up the slope in front of Dillo and shook water all over her.

"Come on, Dillo, it's fun," Ozzy said.

Dillo shook off the water, and looked across the river at Eddy, who was watching the playful fun.

47

"Go ahead, Dillo," said Eddy, "it'll boost your spirits."

"Well, maybe once," said Dillo, thinking that it did look like fun. "Are you sure there are no alligators around here?" she asked.

"No alligators," said Oozie. "Let's go, Dillo."

Dillo followed the two playful otters to the edge of the slope.

Ozzy gave Dillo instructions. "All you have to do is lie flat on your belly and spread your legs out to the side."

"Watch me," called Oozie, as he slid easily down the bank and into the water.

"Me too," said Ozzy, sliding down the muddy bank again.

"Marmma did tell me that armadillos can go under water to hunt for crayfish, but I haven't had my underwater lessons yet," said Dillo, concerned she might not come up after diving in.

"Armadillos are natural swimmers, Dillo. Come on down, give it a try," urged Oozie.

Looking down the muddy chute, Dillo got nervous and excited at the same time.

"OK, I'll try it," she said, feeling butterflies in her tummy.

48

She lay flat on her belly, stretched her legs out from her sides, and looked at the water below.

"Marmma taught us to be brave. I just hope I am wise too," said Dillo. Then she pushed with her hind feet and started to slide.

"**WHEEEEEEE,**" Dillo cried with glee as she slid down the slippery chute. She hit the water head first and found herself on the bottom of the pond. She was surprised that she didn't mind being under the water. She could hold her breath without any problem and just looked around for a minute. She saw several fish skitter by, and some crayfish flipping their tails to get away from her. Then she emerged from the pond to find Eddy, Ozzy, and Oozie together looking at her.

"That was fun!" she exclaimed. "Let's do it again."

The otters were delighted that they had a new playmate. So they played slide for most of the morning while Eddy searched for fish.

After a while Dillo had worn herself out and had to rest. She laughed out loud while watching the frolicking otters play.

Finally she said, "This has really been fun, but I can't play any more. I have to try to get home. I bet my Marmma is worried sick about me."

"OK, Dillo, it's been great fun playing with you," said Ozzy.

"Keep smiling," said Oozie.

"You can count on that," said Dillo, looking at her new friends.

"Come back and play slide with us, Dillo," said Ozzy.

"I would like that a lot," said Dillo. She said goodbye and started walking.

Eddy called from across the water, "Bye Dillo, watch out for you know who."

"Yeah, Snout," said Dillo.

49

- 11 -

Pig Frog

*D*illo was in a very good mood for the first time since Lillo, Pillo, and Jillo had left her. She had had so much fun playing with Ozzy and Oozie Otter. "I hope I meet them again," she thought as she strode along the path.

"Oh good, there's the little bridge," she said to herself. "Uh oh, I hope I don't have to hop over this one."

She walked up to the bridge and saw that the boards were even farther apart than the ones on the big bridge. "Oh, no, I don't want to hop across again."

She looked to the sides and under the bridge. She saw a stream of water going under the bridge to the marshes.

"I can go under the bridge now that I know how to swim," she thought, not thinking of what else might be in the water. She was so excited about not having to hop across the bridge that she just walked off the path and right down into the water. She walked until the water was just her head. She held her breath as she half swam, half walked on the bottom toward the other side. A school of minnows darted over her head. She looked up and saw a black cloud of tadpoles swimming near the surface of the water. She was just climbing out of the water on the other side of the bridge when she heard a loud "**URUMMMMPH.**"

Dillo didn't move a muscle. She saw something green and slippery-looking in the wet grass near the water's edge. Before she could do anything, it jumped out of the grass and landed right in front of her. Dillo's eyes bulged wide open as she stared at the strange creature.

"URUMMMMPH," it said.

"You almost scared me to death!" Dillo said to the huge green frog staring back at her.

"You scared me too," said the frog in a deep, rough voice.

"I've never seen a frog as big as you. Or one with such a loud voice," Dillo said in amazement.

"Yeah, we are easy to hear and hard to find. I am Pig Frog, 'Pig' for short. Who are you? Smiley?" asked Pig with a short croak.

50

"My name is Dillo Armadillo, and I can't help smiling," replied Dillo.

"You can't help smiling?" asked Pig.

"Never mind," said Dillo, tired of telling her story. "I am looking for the Red Mangrove Pond. Do you know where it is?"

"You have found it, Smiley, it is right up the path," said Pig.

"Thanks, **GREENY**, and I am not smiling," Dillo said, now very irritated with Pig Frog for making fun of her. She walked up to the path without saying anything else to that rude Pig Frog. When she got back to the path she heard "URUMMMMPH" behind her.

"Good-bye and good riddance," she said out loud. "What a rude frog. Not everyone is nice in the Bailey Tract."

Pig Frog

- 12 -

Rocco Raccoon

*D*illo looked up ahead and saw another path where she could go either left or right. She walked to the new path and, remembering Oliver's instructions, took a turn to the left. The Red Mangrove Pond was there too. Greatly relieved that she was going in the right direction, she began walking faster. "Marmma can't be very far from here now," she thought.

A little way down the path, Dillo saw something moving on the branch of a buttonwood tree. She stopped short and strained to see what it was. It was as big as Marmma and had a pointy nose. But it seemed to have a fur coat instead of hard armor. It also had a big bushy striped tail. She cautiously moved closer and saw that it had a black mask on its face.

"With that mask, it must be a raccoon. Marmma told me all about raccoons," she thought.

Dillo walked toward the animal hanging from the branch and remembered Marmma telling her that raccoons hunted for food day and night in the Bailey Tract. They really liked to hunt for crayfish and snails. She also said they were quite harmless to armadillos.

When she reached the raccoon, it was looking down at her.

"Hello," said Dillo. "Are you a raccoon?"

"I sure am. My name is Rocco. Nice to meet you, Dillo."

"How did you know my name is Dillo? Dillo asked.

"Eddy Egret told me. I ran into him when I was fishing for crayfish by the river's edge. He told me all about you, and how much fun you had with Ozzy and Oozie Otter. He was right, you are cute, and you don't look sad and lost to me," Rocco said as he climbed down the tree.

"Well, I am not so sad anymore. And I won't be lost for long, either. I think my Marmma is down this path in the woods ahead."

"It must be scary being lost in a strange place," said Rocco.

"Yes, it has been kind of tough," said Dillo, thinking about all she had gone through. "But you know, Rocco, I have learned that being alone isn't all that bad. I've made lots of good friends, and even had fun playing with the otters."

"I can see how you make friends easily, Dillo, with your smile and nice personality," said Rocco.

"Yeah, but I still want to go home and find my Marmma. She must be worried sick about me. At least, I hope she is."

"I'm sure she is, Dillo. I think I can help you find your way back home now," said Rocco.

"Oh, really, Rocco? That would be great. But how can we find her?" asked Dillo.

"Well, I have seen a couple of big armadillos playing in the woods down this path," said Rocco. "And they even dug a hole under a big dead log. Is your home under a big log?"

"Yes, it is, Rocco, but there are so many dead logs in the Bailey Tract. How can I know if it is my home?" answered Dillo.

"This log is a dead cabbage palm tree covered with gray scaly things on it and lots of ferns growing around it," said Rocco.

"That does sound like my home, Rocco," said Dillo hopefully.

"Well, maybe that's where your family is right now," said Rocco.

"Oh, Rocco, please show me where it is," begged Dillo.

"OK, Dillo. Follow me. I think it's a little way past the Red Mangrove Pond," said Rocco, leading the way down the path.

"But isn't that where Snout lives?" asked Dillo.

"Snout lives farther up the path in the big Snout Pond. But don't worry, Dillo, at this time of day Snout is usually sound asleep, sunning himself on the sandy bank of his pond. We'll be very quiet when we go on the path, just in case he can hear us," assured Rocco.

"OK," said Dillo, not fully believing him. She started to walk on her tiptoes.

53

- 13 -
Attack At Snout Pond

Dillo and Rocco walked down the path until they came to a bench at the side of the path.

"Rocco, I think we shouldn't be here," said Dillo. "Oliver said that if I came to a bench by the path, I have gone too far. And Snout Pond is very close to where we are right now."

"Hummm," said Rocco. "Maybe we have gone too far. Let's go back and I'll try to remember where I saw the big armadillos."

They started back up the path when all of a sudden they heard an awful scream coming from the direction of Snout Pond.

*"**HHHEEEELLLLLLLPPPPP,**" cried a little voice.*

"That voice sounds familiar, Rocco," Dillo said, alarmed. "It sounds like one of my sisters."

"*HHHEEEELLLLLLPPPPP,*" the little voice cried again. Then a voice Dillo recognized immediately shouted, "**NOOOOOOOOO!**"

"***Rocco, that's my Marmma!***" Dillo shouted, horrified. And with that, Dillo took off, sprinting toward Snout Pond as fast as her little legs could run.

"**Dillo, DOOOOOONNNN'T,**" yelled Rocco. "**It might be Snout!**"
But Dillo just kept running.

"Oh, no," said Rocco, thinking the worst was about to happen. He swallowed his fear and ran down the path, trying to catch up with Dillo.

Dillo saw the big pond ahead of her. At the water's edge she saw a giant alligator with a long, tooth-filled mouth. "Oh no, that must be Snout," she said out loud. As she got closer, she saw something dangling from Snout's mouth. It was her sister Lillo, hanging by her back leg from Snout's front teeth.

"*HHHHEEEELLLPPP,*" Lillo cried again.

Marmma, not fifteen feet away, screamed, "**LET GOOOOO OF HERRRRR, YOU HORRIBLE BEAST!**"

Without even thinking about the danger, Dillo lunged forward and stopped right in front of Snout's nose. She stood up on all four feet as tall as she could, put her head down, bared her teeth,

Randen T. Eddy

began to raise her head, and roared the loudest roar an armadillo had ever roared. "rrrrRRRROOOOOOOOOWWWWWWWWWWWOOOooo."

Dillo's roar was so loud that there wasn't one animal in all of Bailey Tract that didn't hear her.

Snout stopped moving backwards toward the water and just stared at Dillo. Lillo was hanging from his front teeth, squirming and whimpering in pain. Then Dillo took another deep breath and roared again.

"rrrrRRRROOOOOOOOOOWWWWWWWWWWOOOooo."

At the same time, she slapped her tail on the ground with such power that leaves, twigs, and even stones flew up into the air.

Snout was so totally distracted by the roaring little armadillo in front of him that he didn't see Annie and Arnie Anhinga fly in from behind him. They landed right on top of Snout's head and poked holes all over his nose. At the same time, Eddy Egret flew in, landed on Snout's tail, and began poking him right in the softest part of his behind. Then Ozzy and Oozie Otter sprang up out of the water on either side of Snout and bit into his feet as hard as they could.

"**AHHHHHHHHHHHHHH,**" Snout yelled in pain. When he opened his

Randall T. Eddy

big mouth to cry out,
little Lillo fell to the
ground, helplessly
sobbing in pain.
Oliver Owl, who had
just arrived, flew over
to Lillo, gently picked her
up in his talons, and took
her over to Marmma.

Snout couldn't believe
what was happening to him. He
backed into the water while at the
same time whipping his big head
around in the air, snapping his jaws,
trying to get the big birds off him.
He kicked his feet to get rid of the
otters, plunged into the water,
and swam away as fast as he
could. He looked back to see
if anyone was following him.
Then he turned his head to
continue swimming, and
rammed, nose first, right
into a big log that was
floating in the water. All
of the onlookers at
the edge of the pond laughed and cheered as Snout swam away to
the other side of the pond.

In the meantime, Marmma was licking Lillo's leg wound, and Jillo
and Pillo were licking her face. Fortunately, her wound was not serious
and it looked as if it would heal as good as new in no time.

"Wow," said Gogo, as he plodded up the path to the scene of
chaos. "What's happened here?"

"Yeah, tell me too," said Marsha Rabbit, who hopped up next to
Gogo.

Then Bea and Bob Cat arrived with their kittens. "Is anyone hurt?"
asked Bob Cat.

Everyone gathered around Marmma and Lillo. Rocco began

to tell everyone about the near-tragedy that had just taken place. He finished by saying, "So, it seems that Dillo is our hero. She saved her sister from the jaws of death."

"**DILLO!**" said Marmma looking up from her wounded baby. "Where **is** my Dillo?"

They all looked around. Dillo was nowhere to be seen.

Finally, Marsha Rabbit said, "Look there!" and pointed to a big mound of leaves and grass. They all looked over at the mound and saw a little armadillo's tail, all swollen and battered, sticking out from under the pile of debris.

Bob Cat ran over to the pile and carefully brushed the leaves and stones away with his paw. Dillo just lay there, motionless, with her eyes closed. There was a trickle of blood oozing from the top of her head. But her smile was still on her face.

"**Oh, NOOOO,**" cried Marmma, running over to Dillo. She saw a bloody wound on Dillo's head and began to lick it. "Oh, my poor Dillo," cried Marmma.

Then, to the relief of everyone there, Dillo started to move. She opened her eyes, sat up, and shook her sore head. "Ouch, what happened?" she asked.

- 14 -
The Happy Reunion

"*Oh, Dillo, you are alive,*" said Marmma with great happiness. "*Your poor head, are you OK?*" she said, licking the cut on Dillo's head.

It seems that when Dillo had slapped her tail so hard on the ground in front of Snout, one of the big stones had flipped up into the air and fallen back down on the top of her head, knocking her out.

Dillo looked up and saw her Marmma. "*Marmma, I finally found you,*" she said, cuddling up close to her mother.

Then everyone gathered around the armadillo family and laughed and cheered, joyful that Dillo was reunited with her Marmma.

Dillo stood up, a bit dizzy, and asked, "*What happened to Lillo?*"

"*She's going to be just fine, thanks to you, Dillo. You saved her life,*" said Marmma. She looked with pride and admiration at her smiling daughter.

"*Where is Snout?*" asked Dillo, suddenly concerned.

Rocco spoke up and said, "*After you distracted Snout from almost eating Lillo, Annie, Arnie, and Eddy attacked him with their sharp bills. Then Ozzy and Oozie took care of his feet in true warrior style.*"

"*Yeah, and he screamed with pain and let go of Lillo,*" added Pillo.

"*Right,*" said Oliver. "*And I don't think he will be bothering any of us around here for a very long time.*" They all cheered with delight.

Then Marmma asked Dillo, "*Where have you been? I have been so worried about you. Your sisters said you got lost in the woods when you went off by yourself.*"

Suddenly Dillo remembered everything. She remembered how mean her sisters had been to her. She remembered how scared she had been when she was lost. She remembered all the help she had gotten from all of her new friends. Then she thought she wouldn't have all these new friends, or learned so much about Bailey Tract, and how to express her feelings, if she hadn't been lost.

Dillo looked over at Lillo and asked, "Lillo, are you feeling better?"

"My leg hurts a lot," Lillo said, sniffling. Then she added, "Dillo, I am really sorry that I was so mean to you. You just saved my life. Can you forgive me?"

"Yeah, me too, Dillo," added Jillo.

Then Pillo walked over to Dillo and said, "Dillo, I'm sorry too. We were wrong to be mean to you and to leave you in the woods. Marmma was really upset that you were gone. She made us go out to look for you. But we couldn't find you anywhere and thought you might have been eaten by Snout."

"I guess I can forgive you," said Dillo. "But on one condition."

"What's that?" asked Jillo.

"That you all come with me to the river bank and play slide with Ozzy and Oozie," she said with a big smile on her face.

"Oh great!" they cheered with delight.

"I'm so happy to have my family back together again," said Marmma, as she licked Lillo's leg, and then Dillo's head. She cuddled all four of her daughters close to her.

"Marmma," said Dillo, "I want you to meet my new friends who helped me get back home." Then Dillo introduced them, one by one. She told her all about the adventures she had had with each friend, and what she had learned.

Marmma said, "**Thank you all** for being so nice to my Dillo and helping her to get back to me. Thank you so much, Annie and Arnie, Ozzy and Oozie, and Eddy for bravely attacking Snout. Snout would not have let go of Lillo without you."

"It was Dillo who was brave enough to distract Snout so we could attack him," said Eddy.

"Yes, she did," said Marmma, with great pride in her smiling daughter. "You know you all have helped to make her the true hero she has become today."

"I really think she was born that way," said Oliver. "Just look at her."

They all looked at Dillo and tried to smile too. She was standing tall with her wounded head held high, her swollen tail pointing up in the air, and her big, intentional smile all over her happy face.

The Happy Ending

Dillo's

The Great Horned Owl
22" long, hunts at night for rodents, snakes, small mammals, and birds. It has large yellow eyes and ear-tufts.

The Anhinga
3' long and 3 1/2' wingspan. It spears fish, frogs, and other food underwater with its pointed bill, then tosses it in the air and swallows it.

The Armadillo
The nine-banded is 10 to 15 lb. and is up to 35" long. Bony plates cover its body. It can live up to 15 yrs.

The Bobcat
It is 35" long and weighs up to15 lbs. It hunts for small mammals and birds. It nests in thickets and hollow trees.

The Gopher Tortoise
14" long and weighs 10 lbs. It is a land animal, and digs long burrows. It eats plants, fruits, and grasses. It can live up to 60 years.

Friends

The Florida Raccoon
Weighs 8 to 15 lbs. It eats insects, fish, reptiles, frogs, small mammals, birds, fruit, and nuts. It lives in hollow logs or burrows.

The Great Egret
It is 39" long and has a 4' wingspan. It lives around wetlands and nests in rookery colonies. It eats marine life, lizards, snakes, and frogs.

The Marsh Rabbit
A small rabbit with short ears and a brown tail. It eats plants and grass. It lives in marshy areas and is a good swimmer.

The River Otter
It can be 4 feet long and 30 lbs. It eats mainly marine life and lives in riverbanks. It must be taught to swim.

63

Dillo's Foes

The Pig Frog
It's about 4" long. It eats marine life and insects with its two front feet. It sounds like a pig grunting.

The Yellow Rat Snake
It grows up to 8' long. It eats birds, eggs, rodents, and lizards. It is a powerful constrictor and is not poisonous.

The American Alligator
Grows up to 18' and 300 lbs. It eats almost anything. The mother guards her young with her life.